Spaghetti with the YETI

Adam & Charlotte Guillain

Lee Wildish

SCHOLASTIC INC.

A boy called George had an excellent plan
To go and discover the Yeti.
He put in his backpack a warm woolly hat,
A map and a tin of spaghetti.

Slowly, George climbed up a steep mountain path
In search of the mythical beast . . .

When he stumbled straight into a **monster**
Who was eating a sumptuous feast.

"Hurray!"

shouted George,

"I knew you'd be here.

I'm sure that you must be the Yeti."

The monster stood up with a **furious gaze** ...

"Are you crazy? My name is Betty!"

"So sorry, Betty," said George with a smile,
"But I'm taking the Yeti some lunch."

"In that case you'll want to take some of these bones,
For the Yeti likes food with a **crunch!**"

So George climbed on up the steep mountain path

To track down the hideaway brute,

When he stumbled upon a big monster
With a face like a battered old boot.

"Yippee!" shouted George, "I've tracked you down now,
I've been searching so long for the Yeti."

The monster glared down
with the angriest growl...

"How insulting!
My name is Hetty!"

"So sorry, Hetty," said George with a sigh,
"But I'm taking the Yeti a treat."

"In that case you'll want to take one of these goats . . .

For the Yeti likes food with a **bleat.**"

So George trudged on up the steep mountain path,

Dragging the goat by her tail,

When he spotted a shape in the distance

And heard the most **bone-chilling** wail.

"Hurrah!" shouted George, "At last it IS you.
I've been looking so hard for the Yeti."

The monster looked down with a horrible howl...

"Are you bonkers?
My name is Netty!"

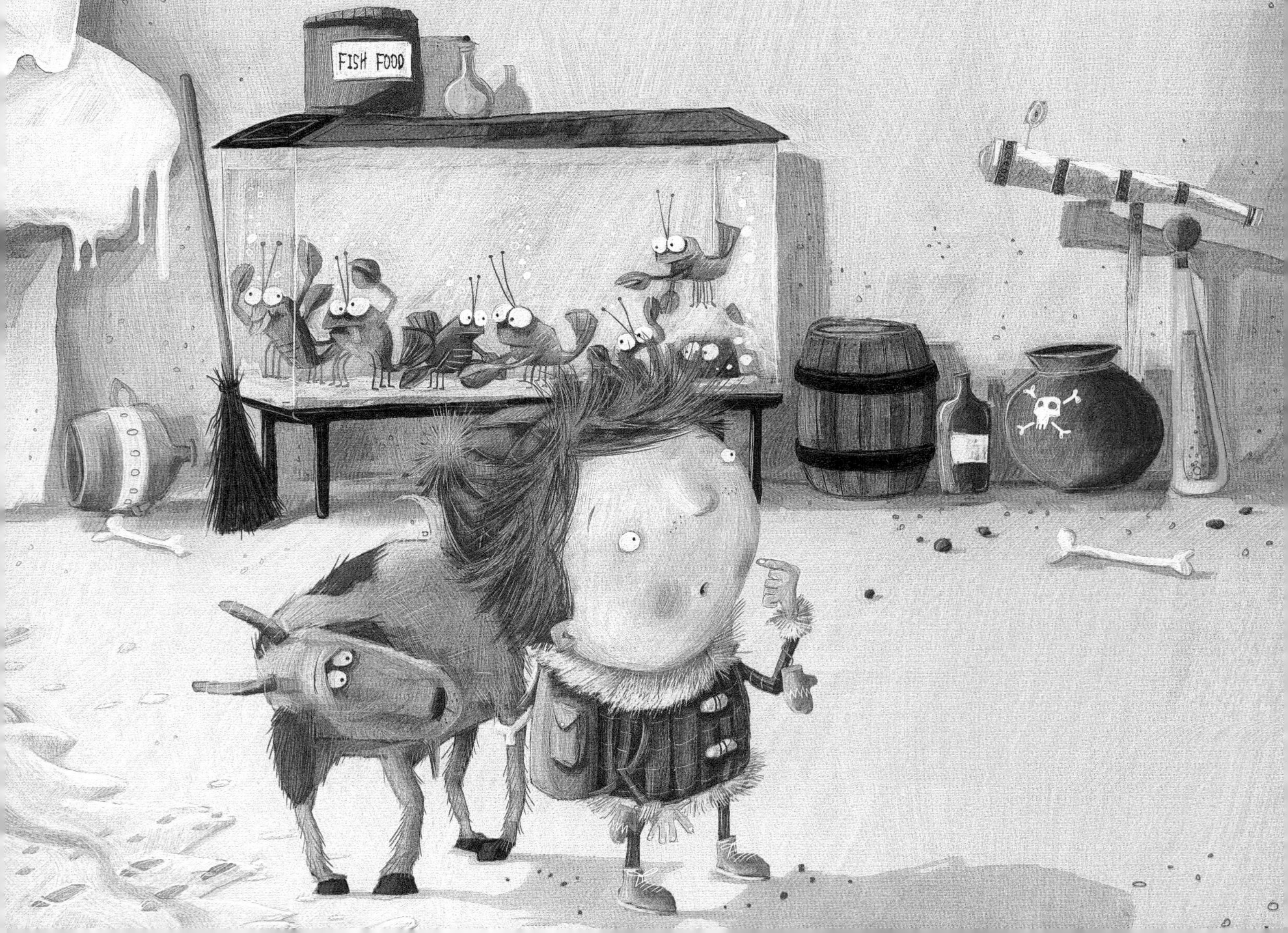

"So sorry, Netty," sighed George, feeling glum,

"But I'm taking the Yeti a snack."

"In that case you'll want to take lobsters and crabs, for the Yeti likes food he can **crack!**"

So George plodded on up the steep mountain path,
The difficult climb made him puff.
Exhausted, he threw himself down on the ground,
"That's it!" he cried, "I've had enough!"

As George sat hopelessly, his head in his hands,
A shadow fell over that place.
He felt something hairy, a prod in the back,
And then turned and peered up at . . .

...a FACE!

"I've found you!"
cried George, with a big happy grin,
And he showed all his gifts to the Yeti.

But the monster looked down
at the crab and the goat
And said, "Sorry, I just
eat spaghetti."

"I knew it!" said George with a whoop of delight,

And he opened the battered old tin.

Then he tipped the spaghetti out into a bowl . . .

. . . and George and the Yeti tucked in.

S
L
U
R
P!

- For our very own George, A&C Guillain -

- For Oscar, Grace and Laura, LW -

First published
in Great Britain 2013
by Egmont UK Limited
No part of this publication may
be reproduced, stored in a retrieval
system, or transmitted in any form or
by any means, electronic, mechanical,
photocopying, recording, or otherwise,
without written permission of the
publisher. For information regarding
permission, write to Egmont USA,
443 Park Avenue South, Suite
806, New York, NY 10016.

12 11 10 9 8 7 6 5

18 19 20/0

ISBN 978-0-545-93149-6

Printed in the U.S.A.

40

First Scholastic printing,
November 2015